Beast Quest®

Skor
THE WINGED STALLION

BY ADAM BLADE

ORCHARD

WELCOME TO

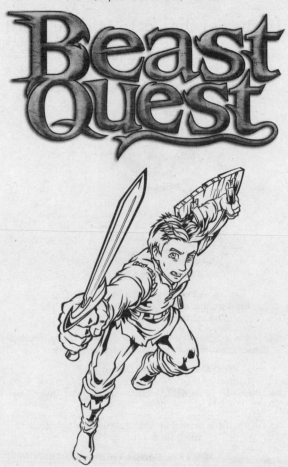

Beast Quest

Collect the special coins in this book.
You will earn one gold coin for
every chapter you read.

Once you have finished all the chapters,
find out what to do with your gold coins at
the back of the book.

With special thanks to Michael Ford

For Connor Kennedy

www.beastquest.co.uk

ORCHARD BOOKS
Carmelite House
50 Victoria Embankment
London EC4Y 0DZ

A Paperback Original
First published in Great Britain in 2008
This edition published in 2015

Beast Quest is a registered trademark of Beast Quest Limited
Series created by Beast Quest Limited, London

Text © Beast Quest Limited 2008
Cover illustration by Steve Sims © Beast Quest Limited 2008
Inside illustration by Brian@KJA-artists.com © Beast Quest Limited
2008

A CIP catalogue record for this book is available from
the British Library.

ISBN 978 1 40834 776 8

1 3 5 7 9 10 8 6 4 2

Printed in Great Britain by Clays Ltd, Elcograf S.p.A.

The paper and board used in this book are made from wood
from responsible sources.

Orchard Books
An imprint of Hachette Children's Group
Part of The Watts Publishing Group Limited
An Hachette UK Company

www.hachette.co.uk

CONTENTS

Welcome. You stand on the edge of darkness, at the gates of an awful land. This place is Gorgonia, the Dark Realm, where the sky is red, the water black and Malvel rules. Tom and Elenna – your hero and his companion – must travel here to complete the next Beast Quest.

Gorgonia is home to six of the deadliest Beasts imaginable – minotaur, winged stallion, sea monster, Gorgon hound, mighty mammoth and scorpion man. Nothing can prepare Tom and Elenna for what they are about to face. Their past victories mean nothing. Only strong hearts and determination will save them now.

Dare you follow Tom's path once more? I advise you to turn back. Heroes can be stubborn and adventures may beckon, but if you decide to stay with Tom, you must be brave and fearless. Anything less will mean certain doom.

Watch where you step...

Kerlo the Gatekeeper

PROLOGUE

Hallam peered through the gloom.
He hardly dared take another step.
Shafts of light danced across the
rainforest floor as the canopy of
leaves swayed above. Who knew
what creatures lurked behind the
thick trunks, or under the giant fern
leaves?

He moved slowly over the mossy
ground. Noises echoed between

the trees – shrill shrieks and low cackles. This place was nothing like the woodland where he and the other Gorgonian rebels used to hide. There, the worst thing a traveller might come across was a wild boar.

But the forest wasn't safe any more. Not since Malvel had closed his net round Gorgonia. His armies scoured the land for rebels, burning the villages of innocent people. There were Beasts, too. Hallam shuddered as he remembered the deaths of his two comrades. Torgor the Minotaur had torn them limb from limb.

Hallam plunged on, flashing glances in the direction of every sound. His sweat-soaked clothes clung to his body. A vine brushed against the back of his neck. He reached up to brush it away, but it wriggled beneath his touch. A snake!

"Urgh!" Hallam cried out, falling backwards.

The snake landed a pace away and drew itself into a coil, hissing. Its scales were a glistening yellow, its eyes blood-red. Hallam lay on the ground, frozen with fear. The snake fixed him with its eyes, its forked tongue flickering in and out, its head swaying, before it uncoiled and slithered away.

Hallam climbed to his feet, brushing wet leaves from his tunic. He pushed on through the trees. "You'll have to more careful!" he told himself.

Hallam was so busy watching the trees for snakes that he didn't notice where he was putting his feet. The next moment he was sliding down a massive slope. The

plants on either side of him were a
blur as he skidded past. And then
he saw what waited at the bottom.

A pit of writhing vipers!

He scrambled to slow himself,
but the mud was too slippery. Vines

broke off in his hand. He jammed his heels into the ground. A hair's breadth from the deadly mass of snakes, he stopped.

The blood thumped in his head, louder than the calls of the birds above.

Trembling, Hallam began to push himself back up the slope.

"You fool!" he muttered to himself. "Malvel's soldiers will find you if you don't watch your step!"

He didn't take his eyes off the snakes. He wanted to get out of the rainforest as quickly as possible.

His back came up against a tree trunk. He gripped the bark with his palms, and then felt something soft, like...feathers. Hot breath misted the air above his head.

Hallam spun round.

A horse's head pushed through the branches above him. But this was no ordinary horse. It towered over Hallam and stared down at him. A Beast! Hallam gasped for breath, his stomach turning over with fear. The creature's lips drew back, revealing a set of yellow teeth, dripping with strings of saliva.

Hallam fell to his knees at the Beast's golden hooves. Huge wings opened from the stallion's body, lifting it above the ground. The creature swayed among the trees, its powerful legs kicking, then it pulled back its head and screeched as Hallam cowered on the ground.

Silver sparks flashed from the Beast's eyes, lighting up the glossy leaves of the jungle, before the fearsome teeth began to close in...

1

VISION IN THE WATER

"We have to clean you up," said Elenna.

Tom and his friend stood beside the river that wound through the dusty Gorgonian plains. It was nothing like the clear streams of Avantia. Here the water was brown and sludgy. Every so often, bubbles escaped to the surface, bursting and filling the air with rotten-smelling yellow gas.

Elenna dabbed the gashes on Tom's arm where Torgor the Minotaur's mighty axe had wounded him. The enchanted talon in Tom's shield, given to him by Epos the Flame Bird, had run out of power before it could heal all of his injuries. It had been Tom's toughest fight yet, but he had managed to free Tagus the Horse-Man from the clutches of Torgor. Now the Good Beast was safely back in Avantia, away from Malvel's evil.

"Do you think the herbs will work?" asked Tom.

Elenna smiled as she ground up

the herbs Tom's aunt had given them. Mixed with some water from her flask, they became a thick paste. Silver the wolf watched as she worked the paste into Tom's wounds.

"Thank you," he said. He didn't know how he would have survived without Elenna on his Quests.

The pain in his arm began to ebb away.

"It's working!" he cried.

The memory of the battle would take longer to fade, though. Torgor was more deadly than any Beast they had faced before. If there were other such creatures in Gorgonia, Tom knew he would need all his strength and courage to defeat them.

Elenna was bandaging the last of the linen dressings over Tom's gashes when Silver leaped to his feet and began pacing along the riverbank, barking wildly at the water.

Tom's horse Storm stamped his hooves and shook his mane, then backed away from the river's edge.

"What's got into Storm and Silver?" asked Elenna.

"Something's spooking them," said Tom. He peered into the water. The current seemed to have stopped. Silver let out a high-pitched whine as a ripple appeared in the middle of the water.

The two friends gazed into the

river as the patterns there shifted.

Gradually they could make out
the lines of a mouth, then a nose,
then two eyes. Ripples like long
white hairs framed the image. The
mouth moved in little waves.

Elenna gasped.

"Aduro!" said Tom.

It was their friend, the Good Wizard of Avantia.

"Greetings, Tom and Elenna," the vision in the water called.

"Greetings," they replied.

"Once again, congratulations on overcoming Torgor," said Aduro. "Tagus sends his thanks from Avantia."

Elenna squeezed Tom's arm, and Aduro continued.

"But, as you know, my magic is weak here in Gorgonia – the gateway between worlds saps my energy. I don't have the power to stay with you long."

"Tell us, Aduro," said Tom, "what is our next mission?"

"You must track down a new Beast," said Aduro. "Its name is Skor."

Tom shot Elenna a look. She shrugged, looking mystified. Aduro's face began to blur at the edges, and his words became distant. His magic was fading. "Beware," he whispered. "I give you a final warning: danger will come from both earth and air. Remember, earth and air..."

The face melted back into the water.

"He's gone!" cried Tom.

"What is Skor?" said Elenna. "How can it be a danger by earth and air?"

"I don't know," said Tom, "but we

have to find out. We already know that Epos is in danger." After the defeat of Torgor, the flame bird's talon in Tom's shield had begun to glow, calling for their help.

Tom picked up his shield, swung it onto his back, and tightened the magic belt around his waist. One of the belt's slots already contained the red jewel he had captured from Torgor. It gave him the ability to communicate with the Beasts. But there were five slots left to fill. Tom wondered what new powers he would gain on this Quest.

"Let's see where we have to head next," Tom suggested.

Elenna opened the bag on Storm's saddle and pulled out the map given to them by Malvel. Unlike the enchanted parchment that had guided them in Avantia, this map was scrawled on animal hide. Tom shuddered as he helped Elenna unroll the greasy yellow surface.

"Look!" said Elenna. "A path."

The stench of the map was overpowering, and Tom held his breath as he leaned in closer. A green line became clear against the discoloured surface. It marked a route from their present location on the plains. The line snaked around steep rocky gullies and ravines, and ended in a place marked with tall trees many miles away. They could see the figure of a tiny flame bird hidden within the trees.

"It's a rainforest! And there's Epos," said Tom.

"It looks dangerous." Elenna sounded worried.

Tom put his hand on her shoulder. "We've overcome thirteen Beasts already," he said. "We can do it if we work together."

"We don't even know if we can trust the map," said Elenna. "Malvel may be leading us to our deaths."

Tom nodded. "Whatever Malvel throws at us, we'll be prepared," he said, rolling up the map. He gazed beyond the river. "Epos needs our help. We won't fail!"

TOWARDS DANGER

Storm galloped across the dusty
plains, Silver bounding tirelessly
by his side. Gorgonia's sun was
hidden behind thick banks of
swirling red cloud, and the gloom
seemed to press down upon them,
ready to swallow them up. The
stallion's hooves struggled to find
a grip on the crumbling soil, and

twice he nearly fell. But Tom gripped Storm's flanks with his legs, watching the terrain to avoid any loose rocks.

"It makes me miss Avantia," said Elenna, over the pounding of Storm's hooves. "This feels like a land of..."

"Death?" finished Tom.

Elenna shivered, as though a chill had run down her spine. There was no sign of life anywhere in Malvel's kingdom, and the stench of decay filled the air. It was as though the Dark Wizard himself was following them, breathing down their necks.

Something appeared on the horizon. Tom felt his heartbeat

quicken. He tightened Storm's reins, slowing the stallion to a canter, and he felt Elenna grip his waist. But his pulse steadied as he saw it was only a dead tree.

The tree looked like a skeletal hand, reaching upwards from the earth. Its branches were leafless and decayed, and a huge vulture with patchy brown feathers perched on one of them. As they trotted past, it swivelled its bald head and fixed them with an evil stare. Tom could feel the scavenger's eyes watching them as they moved away. Silver barked nervously.

"One of Malvel's spies?" Elenna whispered into Tom's ear.

"Who knows?" Tom said, trying not to shudder.

Soon they came to a small watering hole, which looked a little cleaner than the river. Tom and Elenna dismounted and took out their flasks, while Storm trotted over to the water's edge. He bowed his head to drink, then sniffed and neighed. Silver flattened his ears and growled.

"What's the matter, boy?" asked Elenna. Then she spotted something on the far side of the pool. "Urgh!" she cried, and pointed.

A white ribcage, picked clean of flesh, broke the surface of the water. Flies buzzed over it.

"What do you think that was?" asked Elenna.

"I don't know," Tom replied, "but this water isn't safe. I'd rather be parched than poisoned."

Remounting Storm, Tom stroked his mane. "I know you're thirsty, boy, but we've got to keep going."

Storm threw back his head and

shook his mane, letting out a whinny. Tom dug in his heels and the stallion shot forwards once again.

They made good speed across the plains. Ahead, the air shimmered with heat, and Tom could see nothing but pale brown earth, with an occasional spiky gorse bush. But a tingle in his stomach told him something was wrong.

After a while the gorse bushes became thicker, and Tom had to keep his eyes on the ground to steer Storm through safely. He was worried. Was Malvel driving them into the middle of nowhere, where starvation and thirst would wear them down?

"Look out!" yelled Elenna.

Tom saw a cliff edge right in front of them. He pulled back on Storm's reins as hard as he could, and the horse let out a terrified neigh, tossing his head in panic, his hooves skidding towards the edge of the drop and throwing up clouds of dust.

"He doesn't have enough time to stop!" Tom shouted.

They were going over the edge!

INTO THE
GORGE

Storm's body arched under the
saddle as he reared back, his front
hooves wheeling in the air. Pebbles
clattered down into the gulley below,
and the edge of the cliff started to
crumble. Elenna's fingers dug into
Tom's side and he felt his weight
shift backwards. He lost his hold
on the reins. But somehow Storm's

hooves found a grip. Tom heard a thump on the ground behind him, and when he looked he could see that Elenna had fallen to safety.

But twisting round in the saddle made Tom lose his balance. He tried to grab Storm's mane to steady himself, but it was too late. He was falling! The empty valley opened up below him, as rocks and pebbles scattered. His body knocked into the side of the cliff...then pain jolted through his ankle. He was suspended in the air, his arms dangling. His cheeks were grazed by the rough stones, but he was alive.

"Storm's stirrup!" Tom shouted. "It saved me!"

But he hardly dared to move. Only his foot, caught in the stirrup, stopped him from hurtling into the depths of the canyon. Even the magic token in his shield that protected him from falls might not be able to help him in a ravine as deep as this.

Elenna poked her head over the cliff edge. "Hold on!" she shouted.

"I'm not going anywhere," said Tom.

Then he heard her talking to Storm. "That's right, boy, slowly," she coaxed, encouraging the stallion to walk away from the cliff edge and pull Tom back up to solid ground. But he knew they would have to go slowly – Elenna didn't want his foot to slip loose from the stirrup.

Gradually, Tom felt himself being heaved up the cliff. As soon as he approached solid ground, he twisted round and used his arms to scramble to safety. Then he pulled his foot from the stirrup and lay back on the dusty earth, gasping with relief. Silver licked his face excitedly, and he reached out a hand to pat the wolf's neck.

"Thank you, Elenna!" he panted. Storm whinnied. "And you too," Tom added.

The stallion's flanks were slick with sweat and his legs trembled. Elenna whispered gently in his ear, reassuring him. "There, there, boy, it's all right."

She stepped over to gaze down into the ravine. "Do you think anything lives down there?" she asked, her voice echoing among the rocks below.

"I don't know, but we must get across to rescue Epos," said Tom. He pointed to the trees on the other side of the gorge. "That has to be the rainforest."

"Can you jump across, using the power of your golden boots?" Elenna asked.

Tom shook his head. "Here the gorge is as wide as ten houses," he said grimly. "The magic wouldn't be strong enough."

Tom scanned the distance with

his keen sight, one of the powers he had won during his Quest to find the Golden Armour. He spotted something dark looping across the gorge. A bridge! It looked narrow and flimsy, but it was the only choice they had.

"I can see a bridge," he said. "We can cross there."

He swung himself back into Storm's saddle and offered a hand to Elenna. She was pale.

"What's the matter?" Tom asked.

His friend frowned, peering down into the gulley. "We're going to have to be careful," she said. "Those rocks could be deadly."

Tom climbed down from Storm and placed both hands on her shoulders.

"We've battled thirteen Beasts and won," he said. "I know you have the strength to meet this challenge."

Elenna looked up, and Tom saw her face had changed. Her eyes shone with fierce determination.

"Let's do it," she said.

The two of them scrambled into Storm's saddle, and Tom steered his horse in a gallop towards the bridge. Silver's fur flattened as he bounded beside them.

When the bridge drew near, Tom slowed Storm to a canter.

"I've seen stronger bridges!" Elenna joked, trying to smile.

Tom felt doubt tighten in his throat. The bridge that spanned the gorge looked ancient. The rope rails were thin and frayed, and the wooden planks were black with age. Then he remembered the gift given to him by the golden chainmail – strength of heart.

"It's the only way for both of us to cross," he said. "But Storm is too heavy – the bridge won't hold him. He'll have to stay here with Silver."

"Yes," Elenna agreed. Tom felt her

twist in the saddle. "Where is Silver?"

Tom spun round. The wolf was
nowhere to be seen.

"Silver!" shouted Elenna. "Where
are you?"

A howl sounded from behind a
nearby cluster of boulders. They
leaped off Storm, dashed in the
direction of the noise and found
Silver. He was sniffing a bush loaded

with bright red berries.

"Food!" said Elenna. "Clever boy, Silver." She ruffled his fur, then started to pick the fruit.

Tom joined her. It had been so long since they had last eaten. Tom stuffed the juicy berries into his mouth until the sticky sweet juice dribbled down his chin.

"They taste so good," Elenna said with a laugh, licking her fingers. "Who would have thought something so delicious could grow in Gorgonia?"

Tom stopped. Elenna was right. The berries tasted *too* good. He spat out his mouthful, and stared at his friend. Elenna was blurring in front of him. Tom held up his hand in

front of his face – his fingers became
hazy round the edges. He staggered
sideways.

"The berries!" he said. "They're
poisonous!"

It was another of Malvel's evil
tricks, sent to stop their Quest.

Elenna stumbled towards him.
"What shall we do?" she asked.

Tom pointed shakily to the gorge.
"We have to get across the bridge –
while we still can."

Holding onto each other, they
hurried unsteadily towards the edge
of the cliff. Storm came to their side.

"You'll have to stay here," said
Tom, unhooking his shield from the
stallion's saddle and patting the
horse's head.

Silver lifted his nose and licked Elenna's hand.

"You too, Silver," she murmured.

The wolf dropped back, letting out a worried whine.

Tom edged towards the bridge. It was narrow and he felt so unsteady on his feet.

"We'll have to go one at a time," he said. "Let me lead the way."

A strong wind had picked up, gusting along the gorge. The rope bridge swayed and creaked. Tom shuddered. None of his special powers could help him now. He looked back to Storm and Silver. Both animals were watching in silence.

"Maybe we should wait until the

poison wears off," suggested Elenna, tightening her grip on Tom's arm.

"We don't have time," he replied. "Somewhere in that rainforest, Epos needs our help."

"You're right," said Elenna.

Pulling away from his friend's arm, Tom stepped onto the bridge.

1

4

CROSSING THE BRIDGE

"Be careful!" said Elenna. "Don't go too fast."

The bridge groaned under Tom's weight. His vision blurred again, and he shot out a hand to steady himself against the ropes. He managed to take another short step.

Then a screech made him glance up. A black shape drifted under the

clouds. Tom's eyes regained focus.
An eagle! It circled, suspended on
the air, gliding gracefully through
the red sky. It screeched again, the
noise piercing Tom's brain.

Was this another of Malvel's
tricks? A distraction to send him
plummeting to his death?

Tom gripped the ropes and inched
his way across the bridge. Each
time he took another step, the ropes
creaked, but somehow the bridge
held. Tom's dizziness was becoming
worse, though. The wind was
stronger now, whipping through
his hair.

Shaking his head to clear his
thoughts, Tom called back to
Elenna. "It's safe," he shouted.

The wind snatched his breath away. Had she heard him? He yelled again. "The ropes are strong enough! You can come across."

He looked round to see Elenna place a foot on the bridge. So far, so good. But as Elenna took another step, Tom realised he had made a mistake. The bridge began to swing to one side, then the other. The weight of both of them, plus the strong wind, was making the bridge sway dangerously.

Tom bent down, keeping his weight close to the wooden planks. The bridge lurched alarmingly. Was Elenna all right?

He turned round to check. Elenna was making good progress towards him, but the bridge was still swinging violently. Tom began to back towards the end, keeping his eyes on Elenna.

"You're doing well," he called encouragingly. "You're nearly in the middle."

Elenna flashed a weak smile. Then she tripped. She thrust a hand out to break her fall, only just keeping hold of the rope with her other hand. A shudder travelled along the bridge like a wave, tilting it to one side. Tom was thrown against the ropes and cried out in terror. He barely managed to hold on.

"Are you all right?" shouted Elenna.

"I think so!" shouted Tom. "Keep

coming towards me."

He felt something slimy against his palm and looked more closely at the rope he was holding. What he saw made him feel sick. It was made of hair! Many different colours, all wound tightly together. Was it hair from long-dead Beasts?

Or human hair? Who knew what evil Malvel was capable of!

The eagle screeched again, closer this time. Tom watched its black shape swoop low over the bridge. Was it watching them?

Elenna had reached Tom now, and the wind had died down. They were going to make it.

"Nearly there," he said, taking her arm. Then Tom noticed the rope on his left give a tiny shudder. He looked back. The eagle was perched on the far end of the bridge. Gripping the rope between its talons, it tore at the strands with its beak.

"No!" shouted Tom.

Elenna turned round in horror.

Tom didn't have time to explain. Before the eagle was halfway through the twine, there was a loud twang and the rope snapped.

Tom felt his feet fall away and his whole world turned upside down. He and Elenna plunged into the air, their screams echoing through the rocky gorge.

5

ESCAPE FROM THE GORGE

The rock face rushed past. But soon Tom felt himself begin to slow. *Of course! My shield!* he thought. Its magic was protecting him – but would it slow him enough to avoid crashing into the rocks below?

As he passed a ledge, Tom shot out a hand. Jagged rock cut into his fingers, but he held on. His whole body jarred. Elenna was falling towards him, spiralling through the air. He would only get one chance...

He reached out, his fingers closing around her wrist.

"Got you!" he said. The extra weight tore at his muscles, but he couldn't let his friend fall.

Elenna's nails dug into his wrist as she clung to him. Gathering all his strength, Tom heaved her up so she could reach the ledge, then pulled himself up onto it. Thankfully, the evil poison that had blurred his vision seemed to be wearing off and he was able to see what he was doing.

He lay on the ground, panting for breath.

"Thanks," gasped Elenna. "You saved my life."

"How is your eyesight?" asked Tom.

Elenna moved her hand in

front of her face, flexing her fingers. "It's better! Malvel's magic is wearing off."

Tom gazed up. The top of the gorge was far above them.

"How will we get out?" asked Elenna.

"We'll have to climb," said Tom.

But the sides of the gulley were slick with slime. With no ropes, it would be difficult.

Tom hauled himself up against the rock face and placed his foot against a shallow dent. Keeping his body tight against the rock, he began to pick a path upwards, using the tiny crevices to lever his way.

"One step at a time," he called to

Elenna. "Slowly and carefully."

Elenna pulled herself up behind him.

Tom's knuckles turned white, and sweat streamed down his back. He forced himself to concentrate. Reach. Step. Reach. Step. Up there, somewhere, Epos the Flame Bird needed help.

The muscles in his arms and chest ached and his legs shook, but Tom pushed onwards. Then he saw it – a rope. It was the frayed remains of the hair-cord from the bridge, dangling into the abyss. Tom tugged hard on the end. It held.

"We can use this," he called down to Elenna.

He seized the rope and began to

haul himself up, his feet pushing against the slope. Placing hand over hand, he dragged himself up the final section of the cliff. Behind him, he could hear Elenna breathing hard. When he got to the top, Tom leaned back to help his friend. Then they collapsed together in the dirt.

"We've made it!" Elenna gasped.

Tom turned to face the rainforest. Huge trees shot out of the earth. Their luscious green leaves cast the undergrowth into shadow. He could make out vines wrapped around the tree trunks and snaking tendrils hanging from the branches.

"Come on!" said Tom. "Let's make Aduro proud of us."

They hurried towards the forest. Smaller trees grew at the edges, with twisted, leafless branches that seemed to reach out as they passed by. Bushes, sprouting stems lined with thorns, tore at their legs. Parts of the ground were marshy, and Tom felt squelching mud clutch at his feet. Then he noticed something strange. A patch of long swamp-grass was crushed. He walked another few steps and saw another flattened area.

"Look, Elenna," he cried. "They're shaped like…"

"Hooves," Elenna finished.

Tom nodded slowly. "But they must be ten times the size of Storm's hoof-prints! What creature could have hooves that large?"

Elenna didn't answer and Tom shot her a glance. She wasn't even looking at him. Her eyes, opened wide, were fixed on a spot behind his head. Her hand shook as she pointed.

"Skor!" she yelled.

AN ENEMY RETURNS

Tom froze. A horse's body, as black as coal, towered above him. Silver sparks flashed from its eyes. The Beast reared on muscular hind legs, churning the air with gleaming golden hooves. His mane was as white as snow and his tail floated in the air like strands of emerald seaweed.

Skor gave a deafening roar and unfurled giant, glossy wings. He launched himself into the air. Tom staggered backwards into Elenna. The underside of the Beast's feathers shimmered purple like an exotic seashell and the tips looked as if they had been dipped in gold. Tom spotted a shimmer of emerald green in one of the golden hooves. A jewel the size of his fist was embedded there, just like the red gem in Torgor's axe.

Skor beat his mighty wings back and forth, diving low over Tom and Elenna, his huge wings slicing the air above their heads. Then the wheeling hooves crashed back to the ground, sending tremors through the earth that knocked Tom to his knees.

Skor snorted, but didn't come forwards. Then a voice pierced the stillness.

"Very good," it said. "It is right that you should bow before me."

Tom saw a figure jump down from Skor's back. He recognised him right away. The boy was a year or two older than Tom, with pale blond hair. A bronze sword hung by his side.

"Seth!"

"That's right," said the boy. "Didn't you expect to see me again?"

Tom had met Seth once before, on a Quest to save Vedra and Krimon, two baby dragons. But that had been another time, in another kingdom.

"How did you get to—" he began.

"Gorgonia?" Seth finished the question for him. "I'll always be able to find you."

Tom climbed to his feet and drew his sword. *I'll finish the fight this time,* he told himself.

Seth's lip curled into a sneer when he saw Tom's blade. He unsheathed his own. "I hoped I would get the chance to fight you again," he said. Then he turned to Skor and pointed back into the forest with his sword.

"Be gone, Skor! Do Malvel's bidding, and take care of our prisoner."

The Beast snorted and rose into the air. Then it headed back into the depths of the forest, its wing-tips glittering like flames.

Tom tightened his hand around his shield's strap. He pushed Elenna back among the foliage, whispering, "Stay out of the way." Then he raised his voice.

"What have you done to Avantia's Beast?"

Seth laughed. "You won't see her again."

Tom clenched his teeth. "You're nothing but Malvel's puppet."

"That's better than being Aduro's work-horse," Seth shot back.

Tom adjusted his grip, raised his sword and darted forwards, cutting through the air.

Seth stepped aside nimbly, grinning. "This will be easier than I thought," he said.

He lunged at Tom, who parried with a downward stroke. Seth struck again, slicing an arc at Tom's legs. Tom jumped, feeling the draught of the blade pass under his feet. Seth's face was red and he hissed in anger, then brought his blade down heavily.

Tom blocked upwards with his shield, feeling the power of the blow shoot through his arm. Seth grunted. Tom tried to thrust underneath him, but Seth parried, and their blades jammed together. They glared at each other, locked in position, faces close enough for Tom to feel the warmth of Seth's breath.

"You can't keep this up for ever," said Seth through gritted teeth.

"I won't stop until it's over," vowed

Tom, then he thrust his shield into Seth's stomach. They both toppled to the ground, but Tom was up first. "Let your sword do the talking," he said, watching as Seth climbed to his feet, his face dark with anger.

His enemy ran forwards, shouting furiously, and swinging wildly with his sword. It whistled through the air, but Tom kept his shield well placed. He backed away until he saw his chance. He ducked under one of Seth's swings and twisted up behind him. With his right hand he pinned Seth's sword arm. With his left he held his blade to his enemy's throat.

"You've lost!" he said in Seth's ear. "Drop your sword."

Seth's blade clattered to the

ground. Tom kicked it to Elenna.
But as her fingers closed over the
hilt, a high-pitched screech rang
out through the air. It filled Tom's
head and he had to let go of Seth to
cover his ears. He could barely stay
on his feet.

Just as abruptly, the screeching
ceased. Seth was already running in
the direction of the rainforest, but
Tom didn't care about him any more.
He knew that the awful sound was a
Beast in pain. The flame bird's talon,
fixed into his shield, was vibrating
and glowing, and through the red
jewel in his belt, which helped
him to understand the thoughts of
Avantia's Beasts, he realised that
time was running out for Epos.

1

FINDING THE
FLAME BIRD

They dashed towards the rainforest.
Seth had disappeared into the
shadows ahead of them. But Tom
couldn't give chase; he had to get
to Epos.

The trees were massive, the
trunks taller than the towers of
King Hugo's castle and some as
wide as five men.

A figure appeared suddenly from behind one of the trees. Tom recognised his bald head and eyepatch. It was the keeper of the gate between Avantia and Gorgonia.

"Look, Elenna!" he said. "It's Kerlo."

They watched the ragged figure hobble towards them, supported by his wooden staff. Kerlo paused when he was still some distance away. He smiled and lifted his hand.

"Greetings, travellers!" he called out. "How fares your journey?"

"We have to rescue Epos," shouted Tom. "She's trapped in the forest."

Kerlo nodded slowly. "I warned

you, did I not? Gorgonia doesn't welcome fools."

Tom felt his fists clench. "We're not fools, gatekeeper. We have a Quest to fulfil."

"The jungle holds many dangers, young one. You will need great bravery," said Kerlo.

Tom was tired of the gatekeeper's mocking tone. "We're not afraid of anything," he said.

"That's funny," Kerlo replied. "Your father Taladon said the same thing to me once."

Taladon! Tom had never met his father, who had disappeared before Tom was born, but the stories of his brave deeds seemed to have reached the furthest corners of Avantia

– and Gorgonia. Kerlo turned to leave.

"Wait!" said Tom. "Tell me more!"

Epos screeched again, but more faintly this time.

"Come on, Tom," said Elenna. "We don't have much time. She's losing strength."

He nodded. And when he looked back, Kerlo was gone.

They turned and plunged into the foliage. The air in the forest was thick and heavy. It was dark, too, and the shadows shifted as though creatures were creeping through the gloom. Suddenly Elenna seized Tom's arm.

"What's that?" she whispered, pointing.

Tom couldn't see anything but dense leaves.

"What?" he asked.

Elenna relaxed. "I thought I saw something...a pair of eyes."

Tom peered again, and felt a chill tingling down his spine.

"Just stay close," he said.

The ground was covered in spongy moss, and huge fallen branches blocked the path ahead. Mysterious sounds came from all around them – the shrill calls of unseen animals cutting through the air. The leaves above them rustled, but when Tom looked, he could see nothing. Somewhere in the distance a branch splintered. Tom couldn't shake the feeling that they were being watched. But Seth was nowhere to be seen.

"I wish Silver was with us," said Elenna.

Tom thought about Storm, too, and tried to ignore how heavy his heart felt without their loyal friends.

As they moved further into the jungle, the vines became thicker. Tom drew his sword and hacked them aside. The canopy above them blocked out most of the red sunlight. A black shape suddenly broke cover, and shot between their heads. Elenna grabbed her bow and Tom spun round with his sword.

"It's only a bat," said Elenna, relieved. "It won't hurt us."

Epos's cries were fading now, but the talon in Tom's shield vibrated more strongly than ever. If they didn't find the Beast soon, perhaps they never would. Tom couldn't let that happen. *I won't let Aduro down,* he promised himself.

Then his eyes fell on a low branch. It was splintered in the centre, the end hanging loose. He walked nearer. The ground was trampled in the shape of a huge hoof-print.

"Skor must have come this way," he whispered. "Let's follow his tracks – they should lead us to Epos."

They edged forwards, keeping close together. Skor's tracks cut through the forest. Small trees had been torn from the earth and plants crushed.

Soon they reached a clearing. Tom peered between the trees.

"Careful," he said, holding up a hand in front of Elenna. "It might be a trap."

But there she was! Epos the Flame Bird. The Good Beast sat in a makeshift nest of giant leaves. But her feathers weren't the same burnished gold that Tom remembered. They were a dirty brown. And her eyes no longer burned like molten iron. As she shifted in her nest, Tom could see that one wing wasn't folding properly. It stuck out from her body at an awkward angle. From the twisted and missing feathers, Tom realised that the bones must be broken.

"She can't fly," said Tom. "She's completely helpless."

Tears welled in Elenna's eyes. "She must be in terrible pain!"

"It's Malvel's work," Tom said, feeling his anger rise. "And that of his evil helper Seth."

They broke cover and walked towards the stricken Beast.

When Epos spotted them approaching, she lifted her beak and gave a soft caw.

"There, there," said Tom soothingly.

"Do you think the magical talon will be powerful enough to heal her injuries?" asked Elenna.

"I don't know," said Tom. "It's never had to heal anything this bad."

They had almost reached the nest when a rustling came from the far side of the clearing. Tom and Elenna froze.

The leaves began to shake wildly, and tremors stirred the ground beneath their feet.

Golden hooves crashed through

the foliage and giant wings beat
the air.

It was Skor!

8

FACING THE WINGED STALLION

The Beast burst through the trees, cracking small trees like twigs. Epos lifted her head and let out a terrified squawk.

Seth ran out from behind Skor, his sword held in front of him. Tom didn't have time to draw his weapon.

Luckily, Elenna was quicker. She

shoved a foot in Seth's path, and sent him stumbling to the ground. He was climbing back to his feet when she swung a branch at him. It crunched into Seth's temple, and he crumpled to the forest floor beside Epos's nest.

Tom cut down a vine and threw it to Elenna. "Tie him up with this!" he called.

Elenna was on Seth in a flash, and bound his wrists with the vine.

"Quickly, Tom," she shouted. "There isn't much time. The vines won't hold him for long."

A roar filled the clearing and Tom turned to face Skor. The Beast drew back his lips. Huge yellow teeth snapped the air and the

Beast flew up over the trees.

Tom dashed away from the flame bird's nest. He wanted to put as much distance as possible between Skor and Epos.

He was halfway across the clearing when Skor dived at him. Tom ducked and was surrounded by the Beast's stinking breath.

"Over here!" shouted Seth furiously.

Tom spun round to see that Skor's attention had turned to Elenna, who was pinning Seth to the ground. The Beast flew towards her, eyes flashing silver sparks onto the forest floor.

"Hey!" Tom shouted. "Leave her alone!"

Epos bravely tried to lift herself out of her nest, but sank back defeated. Tom picked up a rock from the ground, and took careful aim. Skor was almost on top of Elenna now, and she scrambled back from Seth, who writhed on the ground. Tom threw the rock and it hit the side of Skor's head.

The Beast crashed to the ground, snorting in pain and anger. He charged towards Tom once more. There was no time to think, and nowhere to run. All Tom could do was roll out of the way. He found himself hidden behind a thick tree trunk.

Elenna, meanwhile, had returned to Seth's side.

"Leave him, Elenna!" Tom shouted. "You have to hide."

She looked up, and then back at Seth, uncertainty written on her face. Then she seized their enemy under the armpits and began dragging him towards the edge of the clearing, away from Epos's nest.

Tom heard the crunch of Skor's

hooves in the undergrowth, and flattened himself against the trunk. There was no way he could face this Beast on the forest floor. He wouldn't even be able to get close to Skor's head. Maybe if he could get higher…

Tom looked up the trunk.

Skor appeared at the side of the tree, sniffing the air. The purple feathers of his wings ruffled, and his flanks rose and fell.

Tom edged around the trunk, keeping out of the Beast's sight, then began to climb. The bark of the tree was coarse and cracked, with plenty of handholds, and Tom was as high as Skor's back when the Beast finally spotted him.

Skor's eyes opened wide and

sparks flashed against the trunk,
burning the wood. Then the Beast
opened his mouth and roared. The
yellow teeth snapped at Tom, but
he managed to pull his legs out of
the way. He drew his sword and
swung it at the winged stallion. It
glanced off Skor's head, but did no
damage at all.

"Climb higher!" shouted Elenna.
"You have to get above him."

Tom scrambled up to a hollow

in the trunk, and climbed into it. Skor tried to unfurl his wings, but the trees were too dense. The Beast retreated to the bottom of the tree, out of sight. For a moment, Tom felt safe.

Then the branches began to tremble, as though a strong wind were blowing through them.

"Get out, Tom!" Elenna screamed from below. Tom caught sight of her terrified face through the leaves. She was sheltering by another tree, her foot resting on Seth's back.

Then Tom realised what was happening. The Beast was tearing down the tree!

"You have to climb down!" shouted Elenna.

The Beast attacked the trunk again, and the branches where Tom was crouched shook wildly, scattering leaves below. The whole tree creaked.

Tom sheathed his sword and started to scramble down. But it was too late. The tree leaned over, swinging wildly one way, then the other. Tom felt his stomach lurch.

A loud splintering sound echoed in the clearing and the trunk began to topple, scything through the foliage. Green leaves blurred past Tom's eyes. He had only one chance. He pushed off with his feet and jumped. The ground rushed towards him.

Tom landed on the mossy carpet, bending his knees to cushion the blow, and rolled away. Behind him, the tree slammed into the forest floor. Birds shrieked and dirt filled his eyes.

Skor was already galloping towards him through the debris. Tom drew his sword. He lifted his shield and threw himself at the golden hooves. They thudded against the wood of his shield as he swung his sword, slashing Skor's leg.

The Beast took a few steps backwards – and to Tom's horror, the wound disappeared before his eyes. The skin was unblemished again.

"A Beast that doesn't bleed?" shouted Tom in confusion. "How am I supposed to defeat it?"

"You didn't think Malvel would

make it easy, did you?" Seth cackled. "Face it, you and Epos are going to die!"

"Aim for the head!" shouted Elenna. "It's the only way to stop him."

As the Beast kicked out, Tom dodged sideways to avoid the blow. If reaching Skor's head was the only way to save Epos, that was what he would have to do. *But how can I get close enough?* he thought desperately.

As Skor reared again, Tom saw his chance. He darted under the wheeling hooves and threw himself at Skor's rear leg, wrapping his arms around it. Skor snorted and bucked, kicking out with both his back legs.

Tom felt his teeth rattle in his head, and his sword fell from his grasp.

"Tom!" cried Elenna.

His hands came loose and he was thrown through the air. He smashed into the ground among the leaves of the fallen tree, and a sharp pain stung his forehead. Blood trickled into his eye.

Skor thrashed at the ground with his hooves, then charged towards him, spreading his dazzling wings and lifting from the ground. As he hovered in the air, strings of saliva drooled from his jaws.

"Kill Tom!" bellowed Seth.

"Tom, get up!" shouted Elenna.

Tom struggled to his feet, and faced Skor. The Beast's wingtips scattered golden rays of light across the clearing. Tom looked around for his sword, or something else to fight back with. There was nothing. But Tom wouldn't give up. Not now – not after all they had been through.

As the Beast's hooves sliced towards his face, Tom pushed out his shield. "While there's blood in my veins," he yelled, "Malvel will never triumph!"

1

9

FIGHT TO THE END

Skor's hooves crunched onto Tom's shield, but he kept his arm firm and the wood held. Then Skor whinnied in pain. Tom peered round from behind his shield, and saw an arrow sticking out of Skor's flank.

"Elenna!" he cried.

His friend had left Seth's side and was hurrying towards them, stringing another arrow.

"Run, Tom!" she shouted. "I can't hold him back for long."

Tom looked around. There must

be something he could do.

Elenna unleashed a second arrow, which embedded itself under Skor's mane. The Beast backed off again, but already the first arrow had dropped out, and the skin had healed.

Tom's eyes fell on a reed-filled swamp at the edge of the clearing, and an idea formed in his head. He thought about the way that Elenna had whispered in Storm's ear. Then he remembered a story his uncle had once told him about horse whisperers – people who could calm whole herds of stampeding animals by blowing through pampas grasses. Perhaps the same thing would work with these reeds.

Tom scrambled towards the swamp.

"Stop him!" shouted Seth.

Tom looked back and saw that Elenna was pulling another arrow from her quiver. She only had three left.

The swamp was green and the water was as thick as tar. Tom strode into the centre of the reeking pond. The warm sludge swallowed his legs up to the knee. He tugged at the nearest reed, wincing as the sharp edge cut into his hand. He pulled again, and the reed came free.

"I've got no arrows left!" shouted Elenna.

Skor was thundering towards her.

Tom placed the reed between his hands and blew into his palms.

A note like a shrill scream rang out across the rainforest clearing. Elenna dropped her bow and crouched on the floor, clutching her hands to her ears. Epos gave a cry and sank her head into the side of the nest.

Skor stopped a few paces from Elenna, and lowered his hooves. His eyes sparkled, but no longer sent their lightning bolts into the foliage.

It's working, thought Tom. He took a lungful of air and blew again.

Skor shook his white mane as though getting rid of a nuisance fly.

Then his eyelids drooped and his green tail hung limply.

"No!" shouted Seth. "Curse you both!"

Tom gave a final blow on the reed, and Skor's head sank to his chest. He stood completely still.

"Tom," whispered Elenna, pointing.

"Your sword!"

There it was, resting at the base of a tree. Tom dropped the reed and ran to it. Holding the weapon in his hand, he approached Skor. The mighty Beast towered above him. Could Skor really be asleep? The feathers on his wings didn't so much as stir.

"Be careful!" whispered Elenna.

"I'll have to climb onto his back," said Tom. "I can't reach his head from here."

"No!" shouted Seth. "Wake up, Skor!"

The Beast's eyes shot open, but Tom was quick. He hurled his sword through the air with all his strength. It spiralled towards Skor, the hilt smashing into his head. The winged stallion reared on his hind legs, his mighty wings unfurling and filling the sky with their purple gleam as he shrieked with pain.

Skor's hooves did not fall back down to the ground. He remained frozen, legs raised and mouth gaping, like a statue.

"What's happening?" gasped Elenna.

A green glow began to creep up Skor's back legs. It was as though the forest was reaching out and claiming the Beast. Tom had seen this already with Torgor the Minotaur. As green crystals began to form over the winged stallion's body, Tom leaped out of the way.

A giant emerald prison closed over the Beast. Elenna gave a low whistle of awe. Then Epos sounded a warning squawk.

"Quick!" shouted Elenna. "Seth's escaping."

Tom saw Seth running away, his hands still tied behind his back. Another vine, broken in the centre, trailed from his ankles. Elenna chased after him, and had almost caught their enemy when she tripped and fell into the dirt. Seth took his chance. He dived into the shadows between the trees and was gone.

"He must have cut himself free while I was helping you," said Elenna. "I'm sorry..."

"It's not your fault," said Tom,

placing a hand on Elenna's shoulder. He stared into the forest. "Though I'm sure that's not the last we've seen of Seth."

Together they walked back to Skor.

"What's that?" said Elenna, bending down to pick up something among the long grasses. It was the green jewel from the winged stallion's hoof. "Another token for your belt, Tom."

The gemstone slipped easily into one of the five remaining notches of his belt.

"I wonder what it does," said Tom.

A pitiful wailing interrupted them.

"Epos!" said Elenna.

The flame bird was resting her head on the side of the nest. Short, rasping breaths made her feathers shudder. She stared at Tom pleadingly through half-closed, glassy eyes.

"Quick," said Tom urgently. "We have to help her. She's dying!"

10

A RACE
AGAINST TIME

Close up, it was clear that Epos's
wound was worsening. Forest
insects were hovering over the
bleeding and broken wing.

Elenna stroked the Good Beast's
head. "Can you help her?"

"I can try," said Tom, taking the
enchanted talon from his shield.
He ran it over Epos's injuries but

nothing happened. He tried again.

"Curse Malvel!" said Tom. "It's not working. Perhaps it's just not strong enough."

"Tom!" cried Elenna. "Your belt!"

Tom looked down. Skor's jewel was glowing dimly.

Elenna raised her eyebrows. "Do you think…?"

Tom pulled the crystal from his belt. "There's only one way to find out!"

He held the jewel close to Epos's wounded wing. It shone more brightly the closer it came, until Tom had to shield his eyes. Soon the clearing was completely bathed in green light. Tom watched in amazement as Epos's wing moved a little. Slowly, the bones straightened out as though they were being reset by an invisible hand. Finally, feathers grew back over the bald patch where they had been torn out of the skin.

"The crystal has the power to heal broken bones!" said Tom. "Even those of a Beast!"

Epos lifted her head from the nest. The life flooded back to her eyes as she opened her beak and gave a squawk of gratitude. She spread her mighty wings and a smokeless fire broke out over the feathers. Epos the Flame Bird was alive and well.

"She's more incredible than ever," murmured Elenna.

With a flap of her wings, Epos sprang out of the nest and flew towards the treetops.

Tom looked up at the canopy of branches. "She won't be able to escape the forest," he said. "The trees are too dense."

But something strange happened. As Epos rose up, a slit opened in the air in front of her. It spread until it was as big as Epos herself.

"A gateway!" said Elenna, turning to Tom with wide eyes.

Tom could see blue sky. There were huge towers of stone, too, and flags fluttering in the breeze. He heard the call of distant trumpets. The smell of fresh air filled his nostrils – the smell of home.

"It's King Hugo's castle!" he said, his heart lurching. It seemed so long since he had been home. Epos was hovering by the gateway, ready to leave. At least she could escape the terrible kingdom of Gorgonia.

Tom and Elenna waved.

"Goodbye, Epos!" Tom called.

"It's time for you to see Avantia again." The red jewel in Tom's belt glimmered, allowing him to sense the flame bird's thoughts, and he felt the warmth of Epos's farewell. He knew she was saying thank you. She squawked one final time, and flew through the hole in the sky. It closed up behind her, leaving a scattering of fiery ashes that drifted down into the clearing.

"We've done it, Tom!" said Elenna. "Another Good Beast is free."

Tom nodded in the direction of Skor. "And another of Malvel's Beasts is defeated," he said.

"Where do you think Seth has gone?" asked Elenna.

"I don't know," said Tom. "But

we need to get back to Silver and
Storm. They'll be worried."

Tom and Elenna retraced their
steps. The rainforest didn't seem
nearly as frightening now that Skor
had been defeated.

When they reached the edge of
the forest they could see Silver and
Storm waiting on the far side of the
gorge.

"How are we going to get across?" asked Elenna in dismay. "The bridge is gone!"

The air shimmered and Aduro appeared before them. "Well done, my friends. Allow me to help."

Tom felt himself rising into the air. Beside him, Elenna laughed with delight as they found themselves swooping high over the gulley.

"I feel like a bird!" shouted Elenna.

The ground on the other side was approaching fast.

"Brace yourself!" Tom yelled. He hit the land hard, and sprawled in the dirt. His shield skittered away, and came to a rest against a nearby bush. He climbed to his feet, and looked back over the gorge – but Aduro had gone.

Elenna was still laughing. "I don't think I'll ever be afraid of heights again!" she said.

Storm galloped over and nudged at Tom with his nose. Silver licked Elenna's face excitedly. Tom brushed the earth off his knees and climbed to his feet. It was good to be back together again.

He walked over to retrieve his shield. But as he turned it over, he saw that the sea serpent's tooth on its surface was glowing and vibrating. Tom turned to his companion.

"Elenna, we have to go!" he said.

"Why?" she said, worry creasing her brow.

Tom held out the shield for her to see. "It's Sepron the Sea Serpent."

Another of Avantia's Good Beasts was in danger.

"While there's blood in my veins," Tom swore, thrusting his sword to the sky, "I'll finish this Quest!"

1

CONGRATULATIONS, YOU HAVE COMPLETED THIS QUEST!

At the end of each chapter you were awarded a special gold coin.
The QUEST in this book was worth an amazing 11 coins.

Look at the Beast Quest totem picture inside the back cover of this book to see how far you've come in your journey to become

MASTER OF THE BEASTS.

The more books you read, the more coins you will collect!

Do you want your own
Beast Quest Totem?

1. Cut out and collect the coin below
2. Go to the Beast Quest website
3. Download and print out your totem
4. Add your coin to the totem
www.beastquest.co.uk/totem

Don't miss the next exciting Beast Quest book, NARGA THE SEA MONSTER!

Read on for a sneak peek...

CHAPTER ONE

DECEIVED BY MALVEL

Tom took a short run, pushed off from the ground and soared into the air. Even though he wasn't wearing the Golden Armour, he had not lost its special powers.

But as Tom landed, pain stabbed through his leg. He looked down and saw that a sharp rock jutting up from the ground had torn through his trouser leg and cut his calf. He could have sworn that a moment ago there hadn't been any rocks ahead. But things were never quite as they seemed in Malvel's kingdom.

"What's the matter?" Elenna asked, riding up on Storm, with Silver, her wolf, loping alongside.

"I cut myself on a rock," Tom explained. "I'd better heal it before we go any further."

Tom removed his shield, which he carried over one shoulder. It held the six tokens he had won from each of the Good Beasts of Avantia. Tom took out the talon of Epos the Flame Bird; it felt warm in his hand as he passed it across his bleeding calf. At once, the blood stopped flowing and Tom's skin drew together until there was no sign of a wound.

"Impressive." Elenna smiled.

As Tom replaced the talon, he felt a tingling in his shield. Sepron the Sea Serpent's tooth was vibrating again. The Good Beast was being held captive by one of Malvel's Evil Beasts, and Tom couldn't help but wonder what shape his enemy would take this time.

"Let's get moving," Tom urged, clenching his fists. "Sepron is still in trouble, and while there's blood in my veins, I won't let him die!"

Malvel had dragged the Good Beasts into Gorgonia, leaving Avantia defenceless without its guardians. Tom knew that the Dark Wizard planned to send his own Evil Beasts to conquer the peaceful kingdom.

"Let's have another look at the map," Elenna suggested, "and make sure that we're heading in the right direction."

Tom took the map out of Storm's saddlebag, shuddering as he unrolled it. Malvel had sent the map to Tom and Elenna when they first arrived in Gorgonia. Made from the skin of a dead animal, it smelled disgusting.

Elenna looked over Tom's shoulder as he traced a glowing green line

that appeared on the map. It showed
a route that passed through gentle-
looking fields and ended at the
Black Ocean, where a tiny picture of
Sepron was now etched.

"At least the path ahead looks
easier," Elenna said. "Fields all the
way to the sea."

"Maybe this place isn't all bad,"
Tom said, shaking away thoughts
of the next Beast he would have to
face. "Let's go!" He stowed the map
in the saddlebag again and strode
out confidently along the track.
Elenna urged Storm into motion
and Silver bounded alongside.

As the day wore on, Tom found
that the track didn't take them
across fields, but wound upwards

into craggy hills that grew steeper and rockier with every step. Storm picked his way carefully among the boulders, letting out whinnies of protest when sharp stones stabbed his hooves. Silver whined softly as he tried to find a flat spot to set down his paws.

"I don't understand this," Tom said, gazing around. "Have we come the wrong way?"

"This is the only way we could have come," Elenna replied. "The track didn't divide anywhere."

Shaking his head in confusion, Tom pulled out the map again. "Look," he said. "We should be on flat ground now. The map shows green fields."

Elenna looked bemused. "Why does it show fields if there aren't any?"

"Think about it for a second," Tom said, rage flooding through him as he realised what had happened. "Who gave us this map?"

"Malvel." Elenna's voice was tight with anger.

"Right," said Tom. "We must have been stupid to think we could ever trust it."

Elenna brought Storm to a halt. "We should stop," she suggested. "The map could be leading us in circles."

"There's one thing I do trust," said Tom. He dug deep into his pocket and pulled out the compass left to him by his father, Taladon. He held it in front of him, pointing it up the track.

Elenna leaned over Storm's head to look, and Silver darted around Tom's feet excitedly.

The compass needle was swirling backwards and forwards between *Destiny* and *Danger*.

"Does that mean we'll face both if we go this way?" Elenna asked.

"Yes, it does." Tom stowed the compass away again and straightened up, squaring his shoulders determinedly. "We'll keep going. We have to save Sepron – and ignore Malvel's tricks."

Read
NARGA THE SEA MONSTER
to find out more!

Discover the new Beast Quest mobile game from

MINICLIP
▶ PLAY GAMES

Available free on iOS and Android

  amazon.com

Guide Tom on his Quest to free the Good Beasts
of Avantia from Malvel's evil spells.

Battle the Beasts, defeat the minions,
unearth the secrets and collect
rewards as you journey through the
Kingdom of Avantia.

DOWNLOAD THE APP TO BEGIN
THE ADVENTURE NOW!